For Jack
M.M.

For Francesca Dow
J.R.

Orchard Books
96 Leonard Street, London EC2A 4RH
Orchard Books, Australia
14 Mars Road, Lane Cove, NSW 2066
Text © Margaret Mayo 1996
Illustrations © Jane Ray 1996
ISBN 1 85213 754 1
First published in Great Britain in 1996
The right of Margaret Mayo to be identified as the Author
and Jane Ray to be identified as the Illustrator of this Work
has been asserted by them in accordance with the
Copyright, Designs and Patents Act 1988
A CIP catalogue record of this book is available
from the British Library
Printed in Singapore

THE ORCHARD BOOK OF
MYTHICAL
BIRDS & BEASTS

ORCHARD BOOKS

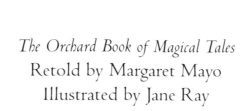

The Orchard Book of Magical Tales
Retold by Margaret Mayo
Illustrated by Jane Ray

The Orchard Book of Creation Stories
Retold by Margaret Mayo
Illustrated by Louise Brierley

The Orchard Book of Stories from the Seven Seas
Retold by Pomme Clayton
Illustrated by Sheila Moxley

The Orchard Book of Irish Fairy Tales and Legends
Retold by Una Leavy
Illustrated by Susan Field

The Orchard Book of Stories from the Ballet
Retold by Geraldine McCaughrean
Illustrated by Angela Barrett

The Orchard Book of Greek Myths
Retold by Geraldine McCaughrean
Illustrated by Emma Chichester Clark

The Orchard Book of Fairy Tales
Retold by Rose Impey
Illustrated by Ian Beck

The Orchard Book of Poems
Compiled by Adrian Mitchell

THE ORCHARD BOOK OF
MYTHICAL
BIRDS & BEASTS

Retold by Margaret Mayo

Illustrated by Jane Ray

· Contents ·

 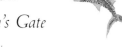

Pegasus: The Chimera

The Horse That Could Fly

Pegasus was a wild and beautiful snow-white horse who had huge feathered wings and could fly. He roamed freely about the land of Greece in the far-off times when gods lived on earth. No one had ever ridden him. No one had even got close enough to touch him, until a certain young prince learned the secret of how to tame this beautiful flying horse.

The prince's name was Bellerophon. He was, of course, a handsome, lively and daring prince, and he loved travel and adventure. But he was not perfect. Who is? Prince Bellerophon's trouble was that he thought rather a lot of himself, and reckoned he could do anything. In fact he was something of a show-off!

On his travels the prince heard about King Iobates, who ruled a country to the north of Greece called Lycia. The king was rich, *and* he had a lovely daughter, *and* he had promised she would marry anyone who could kill a truly awful and ferocious three-headed monster that was rampaging around the country, breathing out fire and destroying everything.

"I shall go to Lycia," Prince Bellerophon thought to himself. "Straight away." And he did.

When the prince arrived, he was welcomed by King Iobates and invited to a feast where all the talk was about the three-headed monster. Nothing else. She was called the Chimera, and she really was weird-looking. She had a lion's head at the front of her body, a goat's head growing out of the middle, while a long twisty snake was attached to the place where a tail should have been. She had lion's legs and claws, but the shaggy body of a goat. Most frightening of all, from each of her three mouths she blasted out fierce flames and vile-smelling poisonous fumes.

"Wherever she goes, she burns and destroys," said the king. "My bravest heroes have gone out to hunt her, but not one has returned. It's impossible to kill the Chimera!"

"There must be a way. . ." murmured Bellerophon, almost to himself. "It must be possible."

The king was annoyed. "So you, my fine prince, are going to rid us of the monster!" he said. "Good! Come back when you've done it!"

And Bellerophon, who was such a proud young man, looked straight at the king and said, "I shall try!"

That night Bellerophon lay awake trying to work out how he could kill the Chimera. "If only I could shoot at her with arrows, from above," he thought. "From just beyond the reach of her fierce flames and deadly breath. If only I could fly. . ." And then he remembered Pegasus. "I must find the winged horse. Catch him and tame him."

Now Bellerphon, like everyone else, believed that the winged horse belonged to the gods. So he took his bow and arrows, boarded a ship and sailed to Greece. When he arrived, he went to the temple of the goddess Athene and prayed for her help.

The prince was tired, so he lay down while he waited for a message from the goddess, and just before dawn he fell asleep. Then he dreamt that a slender woman, dressed in white, stood beside him. In her hands she held a horse's bridle made of gold. "Take this," she said. "With it you can tame Pegasus, who can be found by the enchanted pool which he made with one stamp of his hoof. The pool is high up on the mountain called Helicon."

When the prince woke, he saw, lying on the floor beside him... a golden horse's bridle. He picked it up and examined it carefully, and then, with his bow across his shoulder and the bridle in his hand, he set off to find the enchanted pool.

He walked and walked. He came to the mountain and climbed the slopes, and at last he found a place where cool clear water bubbled up from underground into a pool that was shaped like a large horse's hoof.

Prince Bellerophon sat down, a little way off, resting his back against the trunk of a gnarled old olive tree. He waited, but Pegasus didn't come. It grew dark, and once again the prince fell asleep.

In the morning he was woken by the sound of great wings beating steadily. He looked up, and it seemed as if an enormous snow-white bird with glistening, silver-tipped wings was flying towards the mountain. But this was not a bird. It was Pegasus.

The wingbeats grew slower, and the wonderful horse came gliding down and landed beside the pool. He folded his wings, lowered his beautiful snow-white head and began to drink.

Slowly the prince rose to his feet and with the bridle in his hands tiptoed towards Pegasus. The horse looked up, snorted loudly, stamped his hoofs and spread his wings ready to fly. But then he caught sight of the golden bridle. Immediately he folded his wings and waited, quiet as a lamb, until the prince came right up beside him and slipped the golden bit into his mouth.

The prince stroked the horse's long white mane and gently touched the silver-tipped wings. "Pegasus, greatest of horses," he said, "take me to Lycia and help me kill that dreadful monster the Chimera!"

The prince laid both his hands between the folded wings and jumped lightly on to the horse's back. When he was seated, he took hold of the golden reins. "Now fly!" he called out. And Pegasus spread his wings, slowly beat them up and down, and leaped into the air.

Up and up, they soared together, Pegasus flying faster and faster. How Prince Bellerophon enjoyed himself, riding high in the sky and looking down at the world below! "This," he said, "is the best and only way to travel!"

They flew on, and in a few hours they reached Lycia. At first the countryside below was full of colour, and alive with people and animals. There were fruit trees and vines growing on the hillsides, bright vegetable patches, wild flowers and fields of corn. But before long they came to a place that was utterly destroyed by fire. The grass, the trees, every single plant was black. The houses were empty, burnt-out ruins. There were no men and women, no children, no animals. Everything was dead.

Still they flew on, looking for the Chimera, until Bellerophon saw smoke drifting out from the mouth of a cave. "That cave must be the Chimera's den," said the prince. "Fly down. Let's have a closer look."

Down swooped Pegasus, neighing loudly. And the Chimera heard, gave a long loud lion's roar and came

padding out of the cave. When she saw Pegasus and the prince, she leaped towards them, spouting out long fierce flames and poisonous fumes from her three mouths. The heat was almost unbearable and the smell of the fumes was vile.

But Prince Bellerophon let go of the golden reins and, gripping hold of the horse with his knees, fixed an arrow in his bow, took aim, fired the arrow and struck the Chimera in her lion's throat. The monster roared and belched out more flames and fumes. The prince could hardly breathe, and that would have been the end of him, only the wonderful horse swiftly swerved sideways and flew upwards until they were up in cool fresh air again.

When they had both recovered, the prince urged Pegasus to dive down once more into the smoke and flames. The prince took aim again, and this time he shot an arrow into the monster's heart. She stumbled and fell to the ground, writhing and rolling around, and roaring loudly in her pain and fury.

Then the horse and rider rose up again and hovered in the cool fresh air and waited. After a while the flames died down, the smoke began to clear, and they could see that the Chimera lay on the ground, quiet and still. She was dead.

The prince patted Pegasus fondly on the neck. "Wonderful horse," he said, "our work is done, so take me now to King Iobates's palace." And he shook the golden reins and they were off, flying through the air.

When the prince returned to the palace with Pegasus, and told the king that they had killed the Chimera, there were, as you can imagine, lots of smiles, lots of congratulations and a big celebration feast. Everyone was so glad that the terrible Chimera was dead, and the rest of the country saved from destruction.

And then? Not long after, the handsome prince married the king's only daughter *and* he was made heir to the kingdom! And of course he still had the golden bridle and often rode the wonderful horse Pegasus. So Prince Bellerophon was happy.

And that should have been the end of the story. But — remember — the prince thought rather a lot of himself to begin with and reckoned he could do anything. Well, as time went by, he became an even *bigger* show-off! He would say, "Who killed the Chimera? I did! Has anyone else a horse like mine? *No one!* I am . . . *just like the gods!*"

He couldn't stop thinking how amazingly clever and important he was, until one day he decided to visit the gods in their earthly home on Mount Olympus. So he placed the golden bridle on the horse, mounted, and told him to fly to Olympus.

Pegasus flew up into the air, higher and higher. He set his head towards Mount Olympus, and flew on.

But the gods see everything. And Zeus, king of the gods, was angry. "So this proud young man thinks he is like a god," he said.

And he sent an insect with a very sharp sting, and it stung Pegasus, who was so surprised that he reared up and threw Prince Bellerophon off his back. And the prince fell down a long, long way to the ground — and he died.

But Pegasus continued his journey. When he finally reached Olympus, the gods welcomed him, and Zeus claimed the horse for his own special use.

"Pegasus," he said, "whenever I make storms in the sky, you shall carry the thunder and lightning bolts for me."

And, to this day, Pegasus works for Zeus. So, next time the thunder rolls and lightning flashes, look up, and if you are lucky you may catch a glimpse of Pegasus, the winged horse, flying across the sky.

A Greek myth

The Mermaid

Don't Ever Look at a Mermaid

Once there was a young fisherman called Lutey, and one day he met a mermaid, face to face. Now that's a rare thing to happen to anyone. And it's rarer still to meet a mermaid and live to tell the tale. But he did.

Lutey lived in a cottage overlooking the sea, together with his wife, three lively sons and a large, brown lolloping and most affectionate dog called Towser. And it just so happened that one morning Lutey went for a stroll down on the beach, with Towser at his heels.

The tide was out, and the rippled sands were still wet. The only sound was the lap-lapping of the waves as they rolled ashore. Then, all of a sudden, Lutey heard a strange, mournful cry: "*Aaa-ooooo!*" It was coming from behind some rocks that jutted out into the beach. What could it be?

He hurried forward. Behind the rocks was a shallow pool, fringed by more rocks and separated from the sea by a wide stretch of sand. Lutey gasped. He couldn't believe his eyes. There, sitting on one of the rocks, was *a mermaid*. She was the most beautiful creature he had ever seen. Her skin was white and smooth as marble. She had long golden hair and a wonderful, curving, greenish-blue tail that shimmered softly in the morning sun.

As soon as she saw him, she called out, "Have pity, good man, and help me."

Lutey knew that mermaids were unlucky creatures. He knew the fishermen's saying: "Don't ever look at a mermaid!" But she was so beautiful he couldn't take his eyes off her.

"My name is Lutey," he said, "but who are you? And how can I help you?"

"I am Morvena," she answered. "And I've been sitting here so busy combing my hair and gazing at myself in the water I didn't notice the tide go out. Now I can't get back to the sea unless . . . unless, Lutey, you carry me across the sands. If you do, I'll pay you well."

Lutey laughed. "What can you possibly give to me?"

"I can give you three wishes," she answered.

"Three wishes! Oh! I know what I want! I've often thought about it!" exclaimed Lutey. "Not money. No. Nothing like that."

"Think carefully," said the mermaid. "*Very carefully.* Then choose what you want."

"What I would like," said Lutey quietly, "is the power to heal people when they're sick and make them well and strong again."

"A healer. The gift is yours," she said. "And what else?"

"I would like," he said, "the power to break wicked spells that make folk angry so they end up quarrelling and hurting one another."

"A peacemaker. The gift is yours," she said. "And one more?"

"I would like these powers to continue after I die," said Lutey. "I would like them to pass down through my family, for always."

"The gift is yours," she said. "So now carry me to the sea."

She reached out her white arms and wrapped them round Lutey's neck. But as he lifted her, Towser began to whine. It was a long, low and eerie whine.

Then Lutey was afraid. "How can I know you won't harm me?" he asked.

Morvena touched her hair and took out a golden comb, all delicately patterned and set with tiny pearls. "Take this as a token," she said. And she smiled at him, and Lutey forgot his fear.

"That's a real beauty!" he said as he slipped it into his trouser pocket where he kept various bits and pieces — some string, a pocket-knife and such like.

And then Morvena began to sing. She sang about secret caves and enchanted palaces under the sea. She sang about a life free from pain, death and sadness. As though in a dream, Lutey began to walk across the sands, and his dog Towser followed, still whining. But Lutey had ears only for the mermaid and her songs.

He reached the sea and waded in. But Towser didn't follow. He stayed at the water's edge, still whining.

Lutey waded on, until the water reached the top of his legs. "Now you can swim off," he said.

"Deeper, deeper," sang Morvena. "Take me deeper."

He waded on until the water reached his waist. "Now swim off," he said.

But Morvena only sang, "Deeper, deeper . . . take me deeper."

He waded on until the water reached his shoulders. "I can go no further," he said, and tried to lower her into the water. But she wrapped her arms more tightly round his neck and wound her tail about his legs and sang in his ear.

"Come, come . . . come with me," she sang. And she sang and sang, until the only thing Lutey wanted was to go with her.

And then Towser barked. Again and again he barked, loud and fierce, until the shore echoed with his barking. At last Lutey heard him and looked back and saw his large, brown, lolloping and most affectionate dog by the water's edge. Lutey looked beyond, and saw his three lively sons and his own dear wife standing by the cottage door.

"Let me go!" he cried. "I cannot leave my family and come with you!"

But Morvena only tightened her grasp and tried to pull his head down into the water. Lutey struggled, but though the mermaid was light and seemed quite fragile, her power was greater than his.

But there was still something he could do. He felt in his trouser pocket and pulled out his knife. He flicked it open and held it above the water. "By the power of iron," he cried, "let me go."

Immediately she loosened her hold. "Ah, Lutey," she sighed, "you were cleverer than I thought. You knew that the power of iron is greater than all enchantments." Slowly she swam around him. "Farewell, my lovely man," she said. "Farewell for nine long years . . . and then we shall meet again." And with that she sank below the waves.

Lutey was trembling. It seemed as if his strength had been sucked out of him. But he took a deep breath, slipped his pocket-knife back in its usual place and waded back towards the land.

When he reached the shore, there was Towser lolloping around him, leaping up and licking him all over and doing a lot of tail-wagging. Lutey patted him fondly. "Good dog!" he said. "Without you I would have been lost!"

Of course, when Lutey reached his own cottage, wet through to the skin, there was some explaining to be done.

"What happened?" asked his wife.

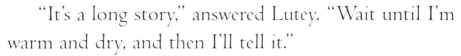

"It's a long story," answered Lutey. "Wait until I'm warm and dry, and then I'll tell it."

A little later, sitting by the fire warming himself, Lutey told his wife and his wide-eyed sons about the mermaid, and at the end he took her comb out of his pocket.

"So the story is true," whispered his wife. "But the three wishes, I wonder, will they come true?"

They did. Lutey discovered that whenever anyone was sick, somehow he knew which herbs and juices and powders to mix together to make the right medicine to cure that person. Even his touch had healing power.

Besides this, Lutey became a peacemaker. Whenever there were quarrels, stealing and fights, people came to Lutey, and somehow he knew the truth and made peace.

News of his gifts spread far and wide, and men, women and children travelled many, many miles to seek his help. And Lutey gave it freely. So he never grew rich. He just stayed a fisherman who loved the sea and fishing, and as his sons grew older, they became fishermen too.

Nine years passed. Nine happy years. But then, late one evening, Lutey went out fishing with Tom, his eldest son, in their small boat.

There was no wind. The sea was calm and still . . . until, without any warning, a gigantic wave came rolling towards them. Lutey and Tom held on tight while it tossed their small boat up and down. Then as soon as the wave had passed, a mermaid rose up from the water. It was Morvena.

"The time has come," she sang. "Now you are mine, Lutey, my lovely man."

Slowly, silently, Lutey rose to his feet, plunged into the water and was gone. And slowly, silently, the mermaid sank below the waves. The last Tom saw of her was her long golden hair spread across the water, and then that too was gone.

Lutey himself was never seen again. But, from that time on, Tom, his eldest son, had the gift of healing, and he too became a peacemaker. And these gifts passed on down, through Lutey's family, even to this day.

But Morvena claims a high price for the gifts. Every nine years, regular as the sea tides, one of Lutey's descendants is lost at sea and never seen again. Perhaps they have gone to join Lutey and the mermaid in the enchanted world under the sea. No one knows for sure.

A story from England

The Unicorn Who Walks Alone

The Unicorn is a beautiful and mysterious beast who always walks alone. He is rarely seen. But once — and *only* once — the Unicorn did come among the other animals. And that one and only time he shared with them his strange and magical powers.

Far, far away there was a wood, and under the shady trees there was a pool of fresh water. It was the animals' pool, where they all came to drink.

Now for months there had been no rain and the sun had shone, hot and fierce. The streams and rivers dried up. The grass turned yellowy-brown. Even the weeds frizzled up and died. But the animals' pool, under the shady trees,

stayed full to the brim. It never failed. And so the animals had enough water to drink.

Until, one day, a serpent came slithering out of a cave. He moved fast across the dry grass, into the wood and straight towards the animals' pool. When he reached the water's edge, he slowly raised his head and, swaying from side to side, stretched over the pool and spurted out a flood of deadly poison. It floated across the surface like oil, covering the whole of the pool. Then the serpent moved off, fast as he came, back to his cave.

And why did the serpent do this? Because he was wicked. Because he felt like it. And because he cared for no one but himself. That was why.

At their usual times the animals sauntered along in ones or twos or friendly little groups towards the pool. But as soon as they reached the water's edge, they smelt the poison and saw it floating on the surface, and they knew that if they swallowed it, they would die.

Some animals were so upset they moaned quietly. Others yelped and roared their anger. Not one turned back and left.

By evening there was a huge crowd round the pool. Animals who were definitely *not* good friends and who *never* drank together stood side by side: the lion, the buffalo and the antelope, the wolf, the camel, the donkey and the sheep . . . and many more besides.

Night came, the moon rose in the sky, and still more animals came. From time to time some would call out and then others would add their voices to the loud, mournful cry. Each time the cry grew louder. Was there no one who could help them?

The Unicorn, the beautiful one who walks alone, was far off, but at last he heard the animals' cry. He listened and understood. He kicked up his hoofs and came trotting, slowly at first, but steadily gaining speed until he was galloping faster than the wind.

As he approached the wood he slowed down, and then, stepping softly, he wound his way in and out among the trees. He saw the animals gathered round the pool. He smelt the poison. Then he knew everything.

The Unicorn knelt beside the pool, lowered his head and dipped his long pointed horn into the water, deeper and deeper, until it was completely covered. He waited a moment and then slowly lifted his horn out of the water. He stood up. His magical horn had done its work. The poison was gone. The water was fresh and pure again.

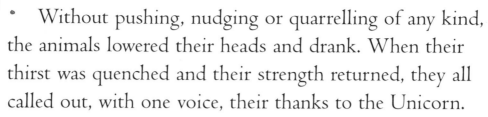

Without pushing, nudging or quarrelling of any kind, the animals lowered their heads and drank. When their thirst was quenched and their strength returned, they all called out, with one voice, their thanks to the Unicorn.

But he was not there. He had left while they were drinking. His work was done. He needed no one. He was the Unicorn who walks alone.

A traditional European story

The Thunderbird

The Green-clawed Thunderbird

Everyone is afraid of Thunderbird. Everyone hides if he comes flying overhead. When he flaps his huge wings, thunder booms. He shuts and opens his shiny eyes, and lightning zigzags down to earth. He can strike trees and break them in pieces. He can strike people, and they die.

But long ago Thunderbird was even more scary than he is now. In those times he had a *terrible, terrible* habit. He stole beautiful girls. Whenever he saw one, he would just swoop down, pick her up in his long green claws and carry her away to his secret home high in the mountains.

One day, in those long ago times, a brave called Long Arrow and his lovely young wife, Red Flower, were walking beside a river when big black clouds came rolling across the sky. They heard the boom of distant thunder, and rain began to fall. And then they knew that Thunderbird was on his way and they must hide.

They ran towards their camp. They ran and they ran, so fast. But Thunderbird was faster. Soon, there he was, overhead, his wings booming out great deafening thunder-claps, while lightning flashed and sizzled all around.

Thunderbird saw Red Flower, and down he swooped. He picked her up in his long green claws, and off he flew.

Now the powerful lightning had stunned Long Arrow and thrown him to the ground. But he was not dead, and after a while he opened his eyes. The storm was over and the earth smelt sweet and fresh. But where was his lovely wife? He looked around. There were no footprints. No signs of her leaving. Then he knew Thunderbird had taken her.

Long Arrow was sad. He turned his back on the camp and walked out to the hills, so that he could be alone. Night came, but he did not sleep. He sat, still and silent, on a hillside, and he thought.

By the time the sun rose in the morning sky, Long Arrow had decided what he would do. He strode back to his tepee and filled a soft leather bag with food for a journey. He took his bow and arrows. He said to his family and friends, "Thunderbird has stolen Red Flower. So now I must find the trail to his secret place, high in the mountains, and make him give back my lovely wife."

All his family, all his friends, said the same thing: "Don't go! You can't save her! If you find him, he will surely kill you!"

But Long Arrow set his mouth firmly shut, and walked off towards the mountains. But he did not know the trail that led to Thunderbird's secret place. He asked every animal he met on the way to help him — the clever coyote, the grizzly bear, the far-flying birds and the fearless wolf — he asked them all. But none of them knew the trail. And they all said the same thing: "Turn back! Don't go! If you find him, he will surely kill you!"

But Long Arrow walked on. He came to the mountains, and still he walked on, until he came to a tepee halfway up the very highest mountain. Raven, the wise one, was standing outside. He greeted the stranger, invited him into his tepee, spread a blanket and offered him food.

When Long Arrow had finished eating, he spoke about his lovely wife and asked Raven, the wise one, if he knew the trail to Thunderbird's secret home.

"You are close," said Raven. "He lives beside the trail that leads to the top of this mountain. His tepee is strange. It isn't made of buffalo skin. It is made of stone, and, hanging from the walls, inside, are lots of eyes, two by two. That is where he hides the beautiful girls he has stolen – in these eyes! Only I, Raven, am greater than Thunderbird and have the power to enter his tepee and live."

"I am afraid," said Long Arrow. "Help me, Raven."

"Take these," said Raven. "They are strong medicine." And he gave Long Arrow one of his big black feathers and an arrow that had a shaft made of elk horn. "If you point my feather at Thunderbird, he cannot harm you. And if you shoot this arrow through the wall of his tepee, you will have power over him."

"I am still afraid," said Long Arrow.

"So – you don't believe in my strong medicine," said Raven. "Come and I will make you believe." They walked outside and Raven said, "Tell me how far you have travelled."

"I was sad, and I didn't count how many sleeps I had on the way," said Long Arrow. "But the trail was long. The berries on the bushes have grown and ripened since I left."

Raven gave him some ointment and told him to rub it in his eyes and then look back towards his home.

As soon as Long Arrow had done that, he called out, so excited, "I can see my camp! I can see the people, the children, the dogs and even the smoke rising up from the tepees." He turned to Raven and said, "Now I am not afraid."

Long Arrow took Raven's feather and the arrow with the elk-horn shaft and walked along the trail that led to the top of the mountain. Just below the peak, he came to what looked like an enormous tepee. But it was made of stone.

Long Arrow entered the tepee, and, though it was very gloomy and dark inside, he could see the shape of Thunderbird, sitting there on the floor. He was huge.

"No one enters my secret place and lives," said Thunderbird, and his eyes began to flash. Then he saw that Long Arrow was pointing Raven's feather towards him. Thunderbird shivered. "You have strong medicine," he said.

"You have stolen my lovely wife, Red Flower," said Long Arrow. "And I have come for her."

"She is mine!" answered Thunderbird. "You cannot have her!"

Long Arrow took his bow and he shot Raven's arrow at the tepee wall. The arrow sped through the stone, making such a large hole that the sun shone in and lit up the place.

Now Long Arrow could see Thunderbird's rainbow-coloured feathers, his curved beak and shiny eyes and long green claws. And he could also see that there were lots of eyes hanging, two by two, from the wall.

"You have Raven's power," said Thunderbird. "So I must give you what you want. Find your wife and take her."

Long Arrow knew Red Flower's lovely eyes. He lifted the string that held them, and she stood before him . . . and she was as lovely as ever.

"Do not come again to my people!" said Long Arrow. "We do not want to see or hear you!"

"But you cannot live without me," answered Thunderbird. "I make the storms of spring and summer. I bring the rain that makes the grass green and fills the berries with juice. Without the rain they would shrivel and die."

"Then come and bring us rain," said Long Arrow. "But promise not to steal our beautiful girls, and try not to harm any of our people with your lightning."

"Take this. It is sacred medicine," said Thunderbird, and gave him a wooden pipe with a long stem that was carved and painted. "When the geese come flying north in spring, you and your people must light the pipe and smoke it and pray to me. And when the smoke rises, I will remember that I must not take your beautiful girls, and that I must try not to harm your people."

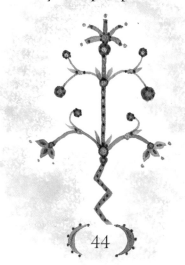

Then Long Arrow took Thunderbird's medicine pipe. And he and Red Flower left the secret place, high on the mountain, and walked along the trail that led back to their own camp. There were many sleeps on the way. But it did not seem far, because they were together and content.

This happened long ago. But still, every spring, the people pray to Thunderbird, asking him not to strike any of their people with his lightning. They smoke the medicine pipe, passing it from hand to hand, and the smoke rises softly upwards. And Thunderbird hears their prayers, and he answers them.

A North American Indian tale

The Fish at Dragon's Gate

There are hundreds of dragons in China. Every pool and river has its own, and there are quite a few more in the sea. They are not fierce, and they don't eat people either – which is just as well, seeing there are such a lot of them. But *why* are there so many dragons in China?

Long ago, in China, there was a flood. It was the same kind of flood as the one in the Bible, when Noah built his big boat. But in China some of the people and animals were saved by two great heroes, some magic clay, and, of course, Chinese dragons come into the story too.

The Yellow Emperor, supreme god of the heavens, was angry. "People keep on doing bad, wicked things," he said. "I'm going to get rid of them! And I'm going to do it now!" So he ordered the rain god to make endless rain.

The rain god was mightily pleased and rushed off across the sky, whipping up big black clouds and throwing down torrents of rain. He didn't stop for a moment. He loved his work.

And so, on earth, it rained endlessly, and there was a great flood. Houses, plants and even trees were swept away, and thousands of people and animals were drowned. A few families ran up into the mountains and managed to survive. But even they were afraid as every day they saw the flood water rise higher.

Only one god – Kun, grandson of the Yellow Emperor – looked down from the heavens and was truly sorry for the people. He went to his grandfather's palace and pleaded with him. "Lord of the Heavens," he said. "Stop the endless rain. Do not let any more people die."

But the Yellow Emperor was still angry, and he simply closed his eyes, drew in a deep breath and turned away.

As Kun walked out of the palace, sadly shaking his head, an old black tortoise came plodding towards him.

"What's the matter?" asked the tortoise.

"I don't want any more people to drown," said Kun. "But I don't know how to help them."

"Magic mud! That's what you need!" said the tortoise. "Just sprinkle some on the flood water and watch what happens next!"

"Where can I get this mud?" asked Kun.

"Easy!" said the tortoise. "The Yellow Emperor has a big jarful in his treasure house."

"But he won't give me any," said Kun. "He doesn't want the flood to end."

"Then . . ." said the tortoise, and he dropped his voice to a whisper, "then . . . you'll have to steal some!"

Kun was a god. In a moment he was inside his grandfather's treasure house. He quickly found a tall jar full of soft greenish clay, took a handful and, a few moments later, was outside again.

He thought, and next thing he was on earth, standing on a mountainside, with that endless rain spattering down on his head. He broke off a small piece of the mud, and sprinkled it on the flood water. It truly was *magic mud*! It doubled in size, doubled again, and yet again. It kept on growing, *and*, at the same time, it soaked up water, like a sponge. Before long there was an island.

Kun worked fast, travelling from place to place, sprinkling magic mud on the water, making more islands and big land bridges between the mountains. People crept out from the caves and huts where they sheltered and watched him. At last they had a little hope . . . maybe the flood would not cover everything.

But the rain still fell, and besides, before Kun had used up all the mud, the Yellow Emperor looked and he saw everything.

"Kun must die!" said the Yellow Emperor, and he ordered the god of fire to do the deed.

When Kun saw the fire god coming, he changed himself into a white horse and tried to hide among some boulders at the top of a mountain. But the fire god hurled a lightning flash, and Kun, the white horse, fell down as if he were dead.

Time passed. Kun, the white horse, stirred. Something was growing inside him. He shuddered, and from out of his body sprang a new life – a golden dragon – young, strong and splendid.

Then Kun, the brave hero, finally died. But his son, who called himself Yu, flew up to the heavens. He entered the palace of the Yellow Emperor, bowed his dragon head and spoke softly and respectfully.

"Great Lord of the Heavens," he said. "I am Yu, the son of Kun, sent into the world to finish his work. Honoured Great-Grandfather, the people have suffered much and are sad. Take pity on them and stop the endless rain."

The Yellow Emperor listened. His anger cooled. "Golden Dragon," he said, "from now on you shall be the rain god. But that is not enough. I must give you some magic mud to make new land and soak up the extra water."

The Yellow Emperor pointed to a tortoise standing in a corner, listening. It was the same old black tortoise who had helped Kun! "You may take," said the Yellow Emperor, and he smiled, "as much magic mud as can be piled on top of that tortoise's back."

Yu, the golden dragon, bowed his head. "I thank you, Great-Grandfather," he said.

There was much to do. Swiftly Yu flew off and broke up the clouds and chased and blew them away. While he was doing this, he came face to face with the old rain god, who was exceedingly cross. He had enjoyed making endless rain, and didn't want to give up his job. But the Yellow Emperor had to be obeyed. All the rain god could do was grumble and complain.

When the rain at last stopped falling on earth, Yu piled some magic mud on the tortoise's back, and then the two of them came down to earth.

And still there was much to do. Yu and the tortoise travelled through the land of China, sprinkling magic mud,

making new land, and at the same time soaking up the flood waters.

When all the magic mud had been used, Yu said to the tortoise, "Only one thing left to do! We must make some rivers!"

Then, with the tortoise leading the way, the golden dragon used his tail to plough deep furrows across the soft muddy soil, from the mountains to the sea.

It was quite easy. There was only one difficult bit. When Yu was ploughing the course of the Yellow River, in northern China, he came to a place where some big rocky cliffs stood in the way. Yu thought for a moment, then he turned round and lashed the rocks with his tail and cut a great chasm through them.

"This place shall be called Dragon's Gate," he said. "It will always be sacred to dragons."

In this way Yu, the golden dragon, made the great rivers which flow across China today. It is said also that when the cold, sad, hungry people ventured out of the caves and huts in the mountains, where they had sheltered during the endless rain, they asked Yu to be their emperor. And so Yu, the golden dragon, became a man-god, and lived on earth.

Yu is still honoured and remembered, especially at Dragon's Gate on the Yellow River. Here, each spring, when the fish swim upstream, they must leap over the fast-flowing rapids that cascade down the chasm which Yu cut with his tail. And the fish that leap through the wild foaming spray and fine mist, and clear the rapids in one

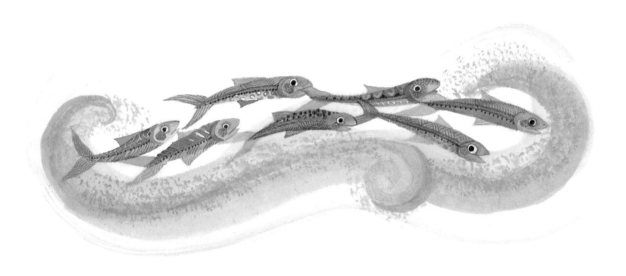

enormous leap — those fish change into dragons and continue their leap up to the clouds. There they frolic and play in the summertime, before returning to the rivers and pools where they sleep in the winter.

Dragons live a long, long time, and every year at Dragon's Gate a few more dragons are born. And that is why there are so many dragons in China.

A story from China

Jamie and the Biggest, First and Father of Sea Serpents

Jamie lived on a farm, not far from the sea, with his mother, father and six brothers. And because he was the youngest and smallest, everyone called him Little Jamie and made him do the boring work no one else would do, like looking after the geese!

One day news reached the farm that the biggest, first and father of sea serpents, Master Stoorworm, had come swimming from the depths of the ocean and parked himself, head to shore and tail to sea, at the next bay along the coast.

Master Stoorworm was immense. His head stuck out of the sea, big as a mountain, his two eyes were like round shiny lakes, while his body was so long that, stretched out, it could have reached across the Atlantic Ocean. Right from Europe to the shores of North America.

The monster's appetite was enormous. But he only ate breakfast. As soon as the morning sun touched his eyes, he opened his wide mouth and yawned. "*Ahhhhh . . .*" he sucked in fresh air, and, "*Hooooo . . .*" he blasted out his vile breath. It smelt like rotten fish. It was a deadly sort of smell.

Six times Master Stoorworm yawned. The seventh time he opened his mouth, he flicked out his long and stretchy forked tongue, scooped up an enormous breakfast and flung it into his mouth. This tongue was so powerful it could knock down a house and grab the people inside. It could sweep up half a dozen cows or a boat full of fishermen. But what frightened people most was that the tongue was so long it was not possible to guess where the monster would strike next.

When Jamie's mother heard about Master Stoorworm she said, "Something must be done!"

"Someone," said his father, "will have to kill him!"

"I'd fight him," said Jamie, who was toasting his toes by the fire. "I'm not scared."

His six brothers laughed out loud and started to tease. "Little Jamie!" they shouted. "Our little brother! The *big hero!*"

Now King Harald, the ruler of that country, was an old man. But he still had a wise head on his shoulders and so he called a meeting of The Thing, which was a council of men who met to make laws and govern. And the king told them that a brave champion must be found to kill Master Stoorworm.

Then there was a babble of voices.

"He can't be killed!" said one. "Waste of time trying!"

"Somehow we've got to keep him happy!" said another.

"We could feed him tasty morsels," said a third. "Seven lovely maidens, tied up on the rocks every morning . . . or maybe a princess. Then the monster would leave the rest of us in peace."

"Wait!" said the king. "Wait seven more days. A champion may be found. And if he does kill Master Stoorworm, he can marry my only child, Princess Gem-de-Lovely, and inherit my kingdom. He shall also have my precious sword, Sicker Snapper, which was given to me by the god Odin himself."

News of the king's prize — a princess, a kingdom and a sword — spread throughout the kingdom and to all the lands about. And so, seven days later, about midday, a large crowd gathered by the seashore. Jamie and his family were there, alongside the king, his lovely daughter, all the members of The Thing, and *thirty-six* tough-looking champion fighters.

Some of the champions had plans, and some had not the least idea what they were going to do. But they all swaggered about looking brave until . . . Master Stoorworm opened his mouth and yawned a sleepy, after-breakfast yawn.

Whew! the smell of his breath was vile. Twelve champions fainted on the spot, twelve were sick and the last twelve clamped their fingers on their noses and ran.

"I see there are no champions left!" said King Harald. "So, tomorrow, before Master Stoorworm wakes, I shall come myself and fight him."

"You are too old, my lord," said his chief steward. "Your fighting days are over."

The king drew out his precious sword, Sicker Snapper. "With thumbs crossed on my good sword, I tell you all," he said, "I will die myself before my daughter or any other maiden is offered to the monster." And he turned to his chief steward and said, "Prepare a boat with two stout oars, mast up and sail ready to hoist, and order the boatman to guard it till I come tomorrow, before sunrise."

On their way home Jamie said to his brothers, "I'd fight Master Stoorworm. Really I would. I'm not scared."

His brothers laughed. "*Little* Jamie! The *big hero!*" they shouted, and, catching hold of him, rolled him on the ground in a rough and tumble — six against one — until their father stopped them.

When Jamie got to his feet, he stuck his chin in the air. "I could have beaten the lot of you!" he said. "But I am saving my strength — for Master Stoorworm!"

That night Jamie lay quietly in his bed. He had made his plans. He was going to fight Master Stoorworm.

As soon as everyone else was fast asleep, he crept outside, mounted his father's horse and galloped off. The moon was full, and the sky starry bright, so Jamie easily found the path that led to the seashore.

When he came to a small, one-roomed cottage, he jumped off the horse, tethered him to the gate post and walked in at the door. Jamie's old granny lay in bed snoring, the peat fire was banked up and on the floor, beside it, stood an iron pot. Jamie bent over, picked up a glowing peat from the fire, placed it in the pot, and crept out as softly as he came. His granny heard nothing. Only the grey cat at the bottom of her bed looked up and stretched himself.

King Harald's boat was ready, mast up and afloat in the shallow water, with the boatman sitting in it, swinging his arms across his chest to warm himself.

Jamie called out, "It's a rare nippy morning! Why don't you take a run on the shore and warm yourself?"

"Leave the boat? I wouldn't dare!" the boatman called back. "The chief steward would have me beaten black and blue if anything happened to the king's boat today!"

Jamie put down the iron pot and began poking around in a rock pool, as if he were collecting shellfish. Suddenly he jumped up and yelled out: "Gold! gold! Yes! It's bright as the sun! It must be gold!"

This was too much for the boatman. In less than a minute he was out of the boat, across the sands and down on his knees by the rock pool, looking for gold. And Jamie? He picked up the pot with the live peat in it, walked lightly across the sands, untied the boat rope, jumped aboard, grabbed hold of an oar and pushed off.

By the time the boatman looked up, Jamie was out at sea, with sail up and flying. The boatman was furious. He waved his arms and yelled the angriest, rudest words he could think of. But there was nothing he could do.

When King Harald, his chief steward, the princess and their servants arrived, they too were furious. And when a whole crowd of curious folk, including Jamie's family, arrived, they were not pleased either. But what could they do? Nothing but wait and watch. Meanwhile Jamie pointed

the small boat towards Master Stoorworm's mountainous head and sailed on. When he came close, he jammed the boat up against the monster's mouth, pulled in the oars and rested.

The sun, round and red, rose slowly above a distant valley. Its bright rays struck Master Stoorworm's two big eyes, and he woke. His wide mouth stretched open, and he began the first of the seven yawns, that he yawned each morning before eating breakfast.

Now, as Master Stoorworm breathed in, a flood of sea water swept into his mouth and down his throat – and the boat and Jamie were sucked in with it. On and on, faster and faster, the boat was swept down and along the monster's throat, which was softly lit, here and there, by a silvery phosphorescent light.

At last the water became shallower and the boat was grounded. Jamie lifted the iron pot, jumped out of the boat and ran on until he came to the monster's liver. He pulled a knife out of his pocket, cut a hole in the oily liver and

stuffed the glowing peat into the hole. He blew and blew until he thought his lips would crack. But, in the end, the peat burst into flame, the oil in the liver hissed and sputtered, there was a flash, and the liver was ablaze.

Jamie ran back to the boat, fast as he could lift his feet. He jumped in and held tight. He was only just in time. When Master Stoorworm felt the fierce heat of the fire inside him, he twisted and turned and threshed about with such violence that he threw up. The entire contents of the monster's enormous stomach came torrenting up his throat, caught hold of the boat, swept it along and along, up and out of his mouth, across the sea, till it landed, high and dry, on a sand dune.

No one took any notice of Jamie! The king and everyone who had come to watch, and that included Jamie's granny and the grey cat who had been woken by the commotion, were all running off to the top of the nearest hill.

Jamie was out of the boat in a moment and soon chasing after them trying to escape the huge waves that were thundering ashore as Master Stoorworm violently twisted and turned.

By now the monster was more to be pitied than feared. Black clouds of smoke were belching out of his mouth and nostrils as the fire inside him grew fiercer. He tossed to and fro. He flung out his forked tongue and stretched it, up and up, towards the cool sky. He tossed his head and his tongue fell down so hard and fast it made a huge dent in the earth and the sea rushed in. And that dent became the crooked straits which now separate Denmark from Norway and Sweden.

Master Stoorworm drew in his tongue, and this time flung his head, up and up, towards the cool sky. He tossed his head, and down it came so hard and fast that some of his teeth fell out and landed in the sea. And they became the scattered islands that are now called the Orkney Isles.

Again his head rose up, he tossed it, and when it came down, a lot more teeth fell out. And they became the Shetland Isles.

A third time the head rose up, and when it came down, the rest of his teeth fell out. And they became the Faroe Isles.

After that Master Stoorworm coiled himself, round and round, into a great lump, and he died. And this lump became Iceland, and the fire which Jamie lit with the burning peat still burns beneath that land. Even today, there are mountains in Iceland which throw out fire.

When everyone was absolutely certain Master Stoorworm was dead, King Harald could scarcely contain himself. He threw his arms round Jamie and called him his son, and he took off his royal cloak and put it on Jamie, and gave him the precious sword, Sicker Snapper. And then the king took hold of the princess's hand and put it in Jamie's hand.

So then there was a wedding – and such a wedding! The feasting and dancing lasted for nine whole weeks. Everyone was so happy because Master Stoorworm was dead and they could now live in peace. And everyone, Jamie's brothers included, agreed that Jamie was their champion and – *a big hero!*

A Scandinavian story told in the Orkney Isles

The Feathered Snake

How Music Came to the World

In the beginning times there was no music on earth. No one knew how to sing. Not even the birds. But there *was* music, far away and high above, in the House of the Sun.

One day the great god Smoking Mirror came to earth and walked about, examining the things he had helped to make.

"Very good! Everything looks just the way I wanted," he said. "The flowers, the birds, the animals! Bright colours everywhere! And yet . . . I feel something is missing." He listened. He walked on and listened some more. "I *know* what's missing," he said.

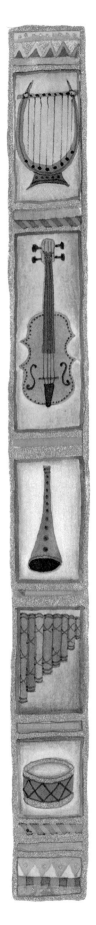

He threw back his head and hurled his voice to the four quarters of the earth. "Come, Quetzal-co-atl, feathered snake, restless Lord of the Winds! Come! I need you!"

Quetzalcoatl was a long way off, drifting lazily above the waves, but he heard. He lifted his snake head and opened his mouth wide, until a human face appeared within his jaws. It was a rather grumpy face.

"It's always the same," he grumbled. "Just when I'm enjoying a rest, I'm wanted for something or other. Still, I suppose I must go and find out what's the matter now!"

He gathered himself together, his glossy feathers rippling around him, changing colour, now green, now turquoise, now blue . . . and then he came flying.

Fast, faster than fast, he flew. Waves rose high. They crashed down on the shore. Trees lifted their branches and tossed them to and fro. In a great whoosh of sound he landed beside Smoking Mirror.

"So – what do you want?" asked Quetzalcoatl. He was brisk and sharp. Those two were not always friends. It didn't take much for them to quarrel.

But Smoking Mirror was cunning. He spoke softly, flatteringly. "Lord of the Winds, there is work that only you can do."

"Wo-rk!" Quetzalcoatl howled out the word. "I wouldn't have come if . . ."

"Listen," said Smoking Mirror. "This bright earth we made together is sick. Listen. Can't you hear? There is no music. And what is life without music? The earth *must* have

music. So, feathered snake, great Lord of the Winds, you must go to the House of the Sun and bring some music down to the earth."

"Go to the Sun! Go and get music!" said Quetzalcoatl. "You know the Sun. He loves music. But he's mean. He won't share. He wants every note of music and every single musician for himself alone!"

"But think of the birds, the trees and the moving water," said Smoking Mirror. "Think of the mothers with their babies, lively children, sleepy children, grown men and women. They must have music. *All life* should be full of music!"

Quetzalcoatl thought. "I will go," he said. "I will go to the House of the Sun." He gathered himself together and flew upwards. Up and up he flew. He soared through the blue smoke of the sky and on through the empty space. He came to the roof of the world, and then he heard the sound of distant music. He rose up the stairway of light that led to the House of the Sun, and the music grew louder and louder, until he could hear clearly the glorious sound of huge choirs singing and sweet flutes playing.

At last he entered the House of the Sun, and saw the musicians.

They circled the Sun in a nest of light. There was not a dark colour anywhere. Each musician was dressed according to the music played. Those who sang lullabies and other songs for children were dressed in white. Those who sang tender love songs wore deep blue, while the ones who sang loud songs about brave deeds and battles were dressed in blood red. But brightest of all were the flute players, who were dressed in a golden yellow that gleamed like the Sun.

The music wove in and out and around the nest of light, as first one group sang and then another played their flutes or maybe sang. The glorious sounds never stopped. Not for a moment.

As soon as he saw him, the Sun knew why Quetzalcoatl had come.

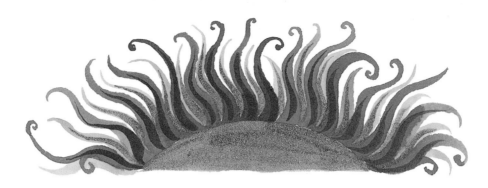

"Musicians, be quiet!" ordered the Sun. "Here comes that bothersome nuisance, the feathered one! Don't answer when he speaks or he will steal you away and take you to that terrible, dark, sad place called earth, where there is no music."

For the first time the musicians were silent. They were afraid, and tried not to listen as Quetzalcoatl drifted among them, whispering in their ears: "Take pity on the people of earth. Come with me, and teach them how to make music. Come . . . come . . ."

Though he pleaded and pleaded, the musicians stood still and silent as statues.

Quetzalcoatl's anger came bubbling up. He coiled himself tight. He uncoiled. He piled up black storm clouds until the Sun's light was covered. He brewed up a hurricane. Lightning flashed. Thunder rumbled and roared.

The musicians were so scared by now! They had never known darkness like this before, and they had never been at the centre of a storm. They ran this way and that, trying to find the Sun, and some, not knowing where they were going, ran straight into Quetzalcoatl's feathered embrace.

When he had hold of some musicians of every kind, he wound his body round them, and slowly and gently, so as not to harm them, he floated down to earth.

Smoking Mirror was there to welcome them as they landed. "Quetzalcoatl," he said, "you have brought such a marvellous flutter of happiness to earth!"

The musicians were so glad when they saw the earth was not a dark terrible place after all. It was full of bright colours, and they could still see the Sun, shining above. It was true there was no music, but they could change that.

Swiftly they walked off to the four quarters of the earth and on their way they taught everyone they met how to sing or how to make flutes and play them.

They also taught the birds to sing, and showed them how to greet the Sun each morning in a loud dawn chorus. They gave music to the moving water and the rustling leaves. They even taught Quetzalcoatl, Lord of the Winds, how to whistle and sigh and sing.

And so now, today, all the earth, everywhere, is full of the happiness which music brings!

A Central American story from Mexico

The One and Only Minotaur

Long ago, on the island of Crete, there lived the Minotaur. The one and only Minotaur. There has never been another. He was a most ferocious beast, half-man, half-bull, and he fed on human flesh.

King Minos, the ruler of Crete, kept the Minotaur in a vast maze called the Labyrinth, which had been specially built underneath the royal palace. It was a terrible place — so dark and such a mass of twisting, turning passages that it was impossible for anyone who went in ever to find their way out again.

At that time, King Minos was all-powerful in the world of the Mediterranean, and in order to feed the ferocious beast he passed a grim law. It was this: every country, across the sea, must take it in turn to send, each year at springtime, seven lads and seven young girls, who would be thrust into the Labyrinth, one by one.

Eight years passed by, and the Minotaur was fed.

The ninth year came. It was spring. The sun shone, the birds sang and the almond trees were pink with blossom. But in Athens there was sadness. The time had come for the city to draw lots and choose seven lads and seven young girls and send them to Crete.

Now Aegeus, King of Athens, was an old man and very frail. But he had an only son called Theseus who was a handsome lad, tall, strong and fast on his feet. And the king loved his only son with a great love.

On the morning when the lots were to be drawn, the king, his son and the citizens of Athens gathered in front of the palace. Some were silent. Some wept. Others whispered prayers to the gods: "Not my son! Not my daughter! Don't let them be chosen!"

When Theseus saw how sad everyone was, he said to his father, "I must go to Crete and try to kill this Minotaur!"

"No – don't go!" said the king. "It would mean certain death. You can't kill this beast alone and unarmed. And even if you did, you'd never find your way out of the terrible Labyrinth."

But Theseus turned to the crowd. "Lots will be drawn for only six young lads," he said. "I shall be the seventh. And, you can be sure, I shall try to kill the Minotaur!"

"Ohhhh . . ." There was a long, low gasp. Everyone was full of admiration that Theseus, the king's only son, should freely offer to go.

When the lots were drawn, and the seven girls and six lads chosen, Theseus gathered the young people round him. "Be brave," he said. "Always have hope. The Minotaur can't live for ever!" Then he led them down to the harbour, followed by their weeping mothers and fathers, sisters and brothers.

Just before Theseus boarded the ship that was to take him to Crete, King Aegeus put his arms about his son. "Theseus, promise me one thing," he said. "The ship is rigged with the black sails of death. Now, if you are on board when it returns, take down the black sails and hoist white ones in their place. Then, even from a long way off, I shall know that you are alive and safe."

And Theseus promised.

A few days later, Theseus and his companions arrived at Knossos, the chief city of Crete. Armed guards met them and took them along steep paths, up stone steps and into the immense royal palace spread out high on a hill.

They entered a beautiful room where every wall was covered with bright painted pictures, and there, seated on his throne, was King Minos with his two daughters, Phaedra and Ariadne, on either side.

Thirteen prisoners stood with their heads bowed. Only Theseus stood, straight and tall, and looked at King Minos, eye to eye.

"Bold youth," said the king, "who are you?"

"I am Theseus, son of Aegeus, King of Athens," he answered. "And I have come to kill the Minotaur so that no more of our young people need die!"

Then the king ordered the guards to search Theseus. And when they found that he carried no weapons, King Minos laughed. "How will you kill the Minotaur?" he asked. "With your hands?"

"If I must!" answered Theseus.

Ariadne, the princess, looked at Theseus. He was so brave, so strong. "I will help him," she thought. "A man like this ought not to die!"

As soon as the young Athenians were taken away to the palace prison, Ariadne went to the kitchens and stirred sleeping powders into some large jugs of wine, and ordered servants to give the wine to the prison guards.

Then she went to her father's room and stole a fine sharp sword.

Finally, she opened a small painted box in which she kept her private treasures and took out a ball of golden thread. This was the ball she had told no one about, not even her sister. It had been given to her when she was a little

girl by clever Daedalus, the man who had designed and built the Labyrinth. He had said, "Play with the glittering ball, Ariadne. But don't forget. It has magic . . ." And he whispered something in her ear.

That night the guards, of course, slept *very* soundly! And so did the prisoners, who were tired from their journey. But Theseus lay awake, trying to work out how he could kill the Minotaur.

About midnight the prison door swung open, and there stood Ariadne, the princess. "Come," she said. "Follow me."

She took him along winding corridors and down long stairways, down and down. At last she unlocked a heavy wooden door and opened it. In front of them was a narrow passage — and beyond it? There was darkness. They were at the entrance to the Labyrinth.

Then Ariadne gave Theseus her father's sword. "With this you can kill the Minotaur," she said. And then she gave him the ball of golden thread, but she held on to the loose end herself. "Place the ball on the floor," she said. "It will roll forward of its own accord, and guide you to the centre of the Labyrinth. When you return, wind it up and it will guide you out."

"And will you wait here till I return?" asked Theseus.

"I shall hold my end of the thread, and I shall wait!" said Ariadne.

Theseus placed the golden ball on the floor and, as it rolled off into the darkness, the threads glowed, giving out a hazy sort of light. He followed behind, along cold, narrow, stone passages. He turned to right and left, twisted back and turned again, on and on, following the ball.

He walked on until the golden ball came to rest in a large, grey, shadowy space. He had reached the heart of the Labyrinth, and there, as if waiting for him, was the Minotaur.

The ferocious beast swung his massive head from side to side. He snorted and stamped his feet. Then, lowering his shoulders, and with his horns, sharp as daggers, pointing forward, he charged.

Theseus gripped the sword and stood his ground. The Minotaur was almost upon him before, in one swift movement, Theseus leaped aside, turned and thrust the sword into the monster's neck. It was enough. The beast stumbled, slowly fell to the floor and died.

Now Theseus had to escape from the Labyrinth. He saw the golden ball shining hazily in a corner. He picked it up and set off, winding the thread round the ball as he went. And the thread led him, by the same twisting, turning route, back to the open door and Ariadne.

Then everything happened quickly. Theseus and Ariadne woke his young companions and guided them out of the palace, and on the way to the harbour Ariadne decided to leave with them. She liked Theseus and wanted to be with him and, besides, she knew her father would be angry when he found out what she had done.

So they all boarded the Athenian ship, the sailors were shaken till they opened their eyes, and the black sails were hoisted. Then — one final thing — before they left Crete, Theseus and the young lads set fire to King Minos's largest and swiftest ships, in case the king chased after them.

After a couple of days at sea a gale blew up and the waves became wild and choppy. Poor Ariadne was seasick and felt so ill the only thing she wanted was to get off the ship. As soon as possible!

She pleaded with Theseus, and in the end he ordered the sailors to make for the nearest island and put her ashore. Before she stepped back on to dry land, Ariadne and Theseus said fond farewells. But that was the end of their friendship. They never saw one another again.

Perhaps it was because of the rough seas and the upset of Ariadne leaving . . . who knows? Anyway, somehow, Theseus forgot his promise to his father, and he did not order the sailors to take down the black sails and hoist white ones in their place.

Day after day, old King Aegeus had watched from the top of the cliffs, waiting for the return of the ship that had taken Theseus to Crete. So, when one morning he saw a ship approaching, with black sails billowing in the wind, he thought his only son was dead. And, overwhelmed by sorrow, the king flung himself into the sea and drowned.

When Theseus's ship finally put down anchor, and he and the six lads and seven young girls came ashore, there was great joy in Athens.

"Theseus, our hero!" the people cried. "You have killed the Minotaur! You have saved our children!" And they hung garlands of flowers around his neck.

For a very short while Theseus was happy. But then a messenger arrived with news of his father's death.

Theseus's eyes filled with tears. "The sails — the black sails!" he said. "Why did I forget?" But the deed was done. It couldn't be changed.

And then Theseus became King of Athens, and he was a good king, wise and strong, and loved by all his people.

But he never forgot his father, who had loved him with such a great love. And, in his honour, Theseus decided to call the sea where King Aegeus had drowned the Aegean. And so it has remained. Look on any map and you will find that the wide waters to the east of Athens are still called the Aegean Sea.

A Greek myth

Three Fabulous Eggs

Once, long ago, the King of the Nagas and his daughter, the Naga Princess, lived in a magnificent underwater palace hidden in a deep lake among the hills of northern Burma.

Sometimes the Naga Princess took the shape of a hooded cobra. Sometimes she was half-woman, half-snake. But she often walked beside the lake or along forest paths as a beautiful young woman dressed in showy, bright-coloured velvet leggings, skirt and top, and with a glorious hood, all set with sparkling rubies, rising up behind her head.

One day when the Naga Princess was walking beside the lake, the Sun Prince glanced down from the sky and saw her. He looked — and he looked again. He couldn't keep his eyes off her.

"She is so beautiful," he thought. "I must speak with her, and find out who she is."

In a moment he came down and stood beside her. The Naga Princess was not surprised. She turned her calm, gentle eyes towards the handsome stranger. They talked together and a strong love grew between them, and before long they decided to marry.

Then they lived together in quiet happiness. But not for long. One morning the Sun Prince remembered that he had work to do.

"I must return to my father, the Sun, and help him light the world," he said. "So come with me, my Naga Princess."

Slowly she shook her head. "I cannot leave these shady forests and my own cool lake. I cannot live in the sky."

"Then every day I will look down and watch you," said the Sun Prince. "And, if at any time you need me, send a white crow with a message." With that he was gone.

The Naga Princess was sad and lonely without her husband, the handsome Sun Prince. Day after day she looked up, and when she saw his father, the Sun, she thought of him.

But then something wonderful happened. The Naga Princess laid three eggs. Three fabulous eggs. They were ruby red, like her favourite jewel, and streaked with gold, from their father, the Sun Prince. She covered the eggs with leaves and guarded them carefully. At last she was happy again.

One morning, when the eggs were almost ready to hatch, she heard a harsh *Caw! caw!* and she saw a crow perched on a nearby tree. He was a white crow, of course, because in those days there were no black ones.

"Crow, will you be my messenger?" she said. "Will you fly up to the sky and ask the Sun Prince to come and see his three children who are soon to be hatched?"

"I'll do that!" said the crow.

"But don't stop on the way!" said the Naga Princess.

"As if I would!" said the crow, and off he flew.

He flew and flew. It was a long way, but in the end he got there.

"Three children! Such good news!" exclaimed the Sun Prince when he heard. "But," and he sighed, "I cannot leave my work. Not now. I'm busy. Still, I shall send my Naga Princess a present."

He searched his father's treasure house until he found a very large, dazzling ruby. "Her favourite jewel — the perfect present," he murmured as he wrapped it carefully in a piece of golden silk and tied up the ends.

He said to the crow, "Tell my Naga Princess that I cannot visit her and my children for a while, but I want her to have this precious ruby as a token of my love."

"I'll do that!" said the crow.

"But don't stop on the way!" said the Sun Prince.

"As if I would!" said the crow, and off he flew.

He flew and he flew. It was a long way, but in the end he reached the hills of northern Burma.

He was almost back home when — *guess what happened* — he saw some merchants sitting on the ground in a forest clearing. They were eating their supper and throwing the left-overs to some birds who were flying around, swooping and diving and noisily quarrelling about the food.

The crow had flown a long way and he was hungry. He didn't think twice. He didn't! He flew down, hopped under a bush, dropped his precious bundle and came fluttering out to join the other birds.

Now one of the merchants had seen the bird drop the bundle. It looked like gold! The merchant hurried over to the bush, reached out, picked up the bundle and untied the piece of golden silk.

"A ruby!" he gasped. "So big! So dazzling! It must be worth a fortune." And he quickly slipped the jewel into his pocket. "I had better put something else in its place," he thought to himself.

He looked around and saw a piece of dried-up cow dung about the same size as the ruby. So — *guess what he did* — he put the dried-up cow dung inside the cloth before tying it up again.

The crow hadn't seen any of this. He was too busy eating. At last, when he was sure he was absolutely full, he hopped over to the bush, picked up the bundle and flew off.

The Naga Princess was so happy when the white crow returned with a small bundle wrapped in golden silk and dropped it in her open hands.

"The Sun Prince is busy," said the crow, who was feeling proud and very important. "He cannot visit you now, but has sent this present as a token of his love."

What could it be? The Naga Princess's fingers trembled as she opened the bundle. She was so excited. But . . . when she saw the dried-up piece of cow dung, she flung it to the ground and her eyes flared with anger.

"Did you stop on the way?" she asked.

"As if I would!" said the crow. He was not foolish. He half guessed what had happened. But was he going to get himself into trouble? Not him. "As if I would!" he repeated, and off he flew.

The Naga Princess, who was usually so quiet and gentle, was full of raging anger. She never wanted to see the Sun Prince again! And the three fabulous eggs? She uncovered them, summoned all her anger into her eyes and glared at them. They were her children. She would not destroy them. She would not turn them to ashes as she was able. But still she glared until all the anger had flowed right out of her and into the eggs.

Then she dived into the lake, changed into a snake-woman and swam back to her father's underwater palace. She had decided never to return to land. From now on she would live in her underwater home.

It has to be said that the Sun Prince was careless. He was so busy working that he forgot to look down and watch the Naga Princess every day. However, a time came when he did look, and he couldn't see her. He looked by the lake and along her favourite paths, and still he couldn't see her.

He looked throughout the land of Burma until his eyes rested on a busy market place, and there he saw a merchant holding in his hands a very large ruby. It was the dazzling ruby that came from the treasure house of the Sun.

The Sun Prince knew immediately that the crow must have stopped on the way. "I will punish him!" said the Sun Prince. He was so angry.

Well, the very first white crow he saw, he blazed fierce sun rays straight at the bird and scorched his white feathers until they turned charcoal black. The Sun Prince saw another white crow, and he scorched his feathers too. *Every time* the Sun Prince saw a white crow he did the same thing.

And that is why there are no longer any white crows in Burma. They are all charcoal black.

Now, you must wonder, *what happened to the three fabulous eggs?*

They just lay where the Naga Princess had left them until the rainy season came. Then water came gushing down the hillside and washed the three eggs into a stream, and the stream carried them into a big river, where they were bounced and tossed and swept along by the swirling water.

When they reached the town of Mogok, one of the eggs was flung against a rock. It burst open . . . *and hundreds of dazzling rubies came cascading out.* And, from that day to this, rubies are to be found near the town of Mogok.

The two remaining eggs were swept along into the great Irawaddy River, and there one of the eggs was flung against a rock. It burst open . . . *and a tiger came leaping and snarling out of the egg.* And, from that day to this, the most ferocious tigers in the world are to be found in the jungles of Burma.

The remaining egg was swept along and, just before the Irawaddy River reaches the sea, this egg was flung against a rock. It burst open . . . *and a crocodile came crawling out, snapping his jaws.* And, from that day to this, hungry crocodiles are to be found lurking in all the shallow creeks and rivers of Lower Burma.

So it is that the rubies, the tigers and the crocodiles of Burma are brothers and sisters. They are all the children of the Sun Prince and his beautiful wife, the Naga Princess.

A story from Burma

The Phoenix

Bird of the Sun

There is a bird that lays no eggs and has no young. It was here when things began and is still living today, in a hidden, faraway desert place. It is the Phoenix, the bird of fire.

One day, in the beginning times, the Sun looked down and saw a large bird with the most beautiful shiny feathers. They were red, gold, purple – bright and dazzling like the Sun itself. The Sun called out, "Glorious Phoenix, you shall be my bird and live for ever!"

Live for ever! The Phoenix was really happy when it heard this, and it lifted its head and sang, "Sun, glorious Sun, I shall sing my songs for you alone!"

But the Phoenix was not happy for long. Poor bird. Its feathers were far too beautiful. Men, women and children were always chasing it and trying to trap it. They wanted to have some of those shiny feathers for themselves.

"I cannot live here," thought the Phoenix. And it flew off towards the east, where the Sun rises in the morning.

The Phoenix flew and it flew, until it came to a faraway, hidden desert where there were no humans. And there it lived in peace, flying freely and singing its songs of praise to the Sun above.

Almost five hundred years passed by. The Phoenix was still alive, but it had grown old. It was often tired, and it had lost much of its strength. It couldn't soar so high in the sky, nor fly as fast or as far as when it was young.

"I don't want to live like this," thought the Phoenix. "I want to be young and strong."

So the Phoenix lifted its head and sang, "Sun, glorious Sun, make me young and strong again!" But the Sun didn't answer. Day after day the Phoenix sang. But when the Sun still didn't answer, the Phoenix decided to return to the place where it had lived in the beginning, and ask the Sun one more time.

It flew across the desert, and over hills, green valleys and high mountains. It was a long journey, and because the Phoenix was old and weak, it had to rest on the way. Now the Phoenix has a keen sense of smell, and is particularly fond of herbs and spices. So, each time it landed, it collected pieces of cinnamon bark and all kinds of fragrant leaves. And it tucked some in amongst its feathers and carried the rest in its claws.

When the bird came at last to the place which had once been its home, it landed on a tall palm tree that was growing high on a mountainside. And, right at the top of the tree, the Phoenix built a nest with the cinnamon bark and lined it with the fragrant leaves. Then the Phoenix flew off and collected some of that sharp-scented gum called myrrh, which it had seen oozing out of a tree close by, and made an egg from the myrrh, and carried the egg back to the nest.

Now everything was ready. The Phoenix sat down in its nest, lifted its head and sang, "Sun, glorious Sun, make me young and strong again!"

This time the Sun heard the song. Swiftly it chased the clouds from the sky and stilled the winds and shone down on the mountainside with all its power.

The animals, the snakes, the lizards and every other bird hid from the Sun's fierce rays, in caves and holes, under shady rocks and trees. Only the Phoenix sat upon its nest and let the Sun's rays beat down upon its beautiful shiny feathers.

Suddenly there was a flash of light, flames leapt out of the nest and the Phoenix became a big round blaze of fire.

After a while the flames died down. The tree was not burnt, nor was the nest. But the Phoenix was gone and in the nest was a heap of silvery-grey ash.

The ash began to tremble and slowly heave itself upward . . . and from under the ash there rose up a young Phoenix. It was small and looked sort of crumpled. But it stretched its neck and lifted its wings and flapped them. Moment by moment it grew, until it was the same size as the old Phoenix. It looked around and found the egg made of myrrh, hollowed it out, placed the ashes inside and finally closed up the egg. And then the Phoenix lifted its head and sang, "Sun, glorious Sun, I shall sing my songs for you alone! For ever and ever!"

When the song ended, the wind began to blow, the clouds came scudding across the sky, and the other living creatures crept out of their hiding places.

Then the Phoenix, with the egg in its claws, flew up and away. At the same time a cloud of birds, of all shapes and sizes, rose up from the earth and flew behind the Phoenix, singing together, "You are the greatest of birds! You are our king!"

And the birds flew with the Phoenix to the temple of the Sun which the Egyptians had built at Heliopolis, City of the Sun. Then the Phoenix placed the egg, with the ashes inside, on the Sun's altar.

"Now," said the Phoenix, "I must fly on alone." And, watched by the other birds, it flew off towards the faraway desert.

The Phoenix lives there still. But every five hundred years, when it begins to feel weak and old, it flies west to the same mountain. There it builds a fragrant nest, on top of a palm tree, and once again it is burnt to ashes. But the Phoenix always rises up from those ashes, fresh and new and young again.

An Egyptian story

· More About ·
· the Stories ·

The Horse That Could Fly

Sometimes the fire-breathing Chimera is described as having just two heads — a lion's and a snake's — on a goat's body. Even still, she is such an unlikely-looking creature that her name is used in the English language to describe a wild, foolish dream or fancy. In Greek myths she has two equally strange sisters. One, Cerberus, a three-headed hound with a snake tail, guards Hades, Land of the Dead. The other, the Hydra, is a water monster who has a whole lot of snaky heads. The big problem is, if one head is cut off, another two or maybe three sprout up in its place. See Robert Graves, *The Greek Myths* (2 vols.), 1955.

The great mass of wonderful stories we call Greek myths were first written down over two and a half thousand years ago. But some of the stories and some of the fabulous beasts, such as the winged horse and the Chimera, have their origins in earlier civilizations of the Near East.

Don't Ever Look at a Mermaid

Reported sightings of a real, live Mermaid were quite common among European sailors right up to about a hundred years ago. She was usually sitting alone on a rock, combing her long flowing hair, or swimming among the waves.

The Mermaid is always dangerous. She can easily bewitch a man with her beauty and sweet singing, and then lure him to her underwater home, a place full of treasures. Mermen, on the other hand, are cross and ugly, not particularly interested in humans and not often seen. But if a Mermaid is harmed, Mermen will raise storms and wreck ships.

This story is retold from Robert Hunt, *Popular Romances of the West of England*, 1865, and William Bottrell, *Traditional and Hearthside Stories of West Cornwall*, 1870.

The Unicorn Who Walks Alone

The earliest surviving description of a Unicorn was written about 400 BC by Ctesias, a Greek physician, who had travelled with the King of Persia. He wrote that, in India, there were swift wild asses with white bodies, dark red heads and a pointed horn on the middle of the forehead. This horn was about half a metre long, white at the base, black in the middle and bright crimson at the top. Any cup made from the horn would protect the drinker from poison. During the Middle Ages, particularly in Western Europe, belief that the horn could be used against poison resulted in a lively trade in what were thought to be Unicorn horns. Most of these were probably tusks of a sea mammal, the narwhal. In 1605 one horn was bought for 12,000 gold pieces.

This story began its life in a bestiary — a book of facts and fables about real and imaginary animals. Bestiaries were popular with Christians from about the third century onwards. The story is retold from Odell Shepard, *The Lore of the Unicorn*, 1930.

Over the centuries, writers and, more especially, artists have changed the Unicorn. He has become all white, more goat-like and less horse-like. The horn has grown longer, changed to black, then white, and developed spiral markings.

The Green-clawed Thunderbird

The idea that thunder was caused by a bird flapping its great wings, and lightning by its blinking an eye was widespread among North American Indian tribes of the Pacific North-west, and in the plateaux, the plains and north-eastern woodlands.

Some believed there was a flock or family of thunderbirds, while others believed there was one enormous bird. Along the Pacific coast, it was thought to be so strong it could lift a large whale out of the ocean and carry it ashore. According to a tradition of the Blackfoot (a northern plains tribe), a thunderbird was once overcome by a snowstorm and landed in a camp, and the people saw that its feathers had many colours, like the rainbow, and its claws were long and green.

The story is retold from G. B. Grinnell, *Blackfoot Lodge Tales*, 1893.

The Fish at Dragon's Gate

The Chinese dragon has a head like a camel, two horns, whiskers at the sides of its mouth and carries a precious pearl under its chin or in its mouth. Like the European folktale dragon, it has scales, four legs, claws, a hoard of treasure and it can fly. But it usually has no wings, it does not eat beautiful young girls, and it breathes out misty clouds, not fire or deadly fumes. It sleeps in pools, rivers or even the sea in winter. In spring it wakes and flies up to the sky, where all dragons gather to fight and play and make the summer rain. Sometimes they stay up too long, and the rains are then so heavy that there are floods.

The story is based on material in Yüan Ke (selected and translated by K. Echlin and N. Zhixiong), *Dragons and Dynasties: An Introduction to Chinese Mythology*, 1993, and Anne Birrell, *Chinese Mythology: An Introduction*, 1993.

Jamie and the Biggest, First and Father of Sea Serpents

According to Scandinavian mythology, an immense serpent lies beneath the sea, curled around the earth, tail in mouth. It will break loose when the world ends. Then Thor, god of thunder, will fight it, but fate has decided that the serpent's poisonous fumes will finally kill the god.

The story of Master Stoorworm comes from the Orkney Isles, which, like the Shetland Isles, have a rich heritage of stories and beliefs from their long Scandinavian past. Although now part of Scotland, until the second half of the fifteenth century both sets of islands owed allegiance to the King of Norway, and Norn rather than Lowland Scots was still the main spoken language.

In the Shetland Isles there was a belief that, way out at sea, lived a serpent that took six hours to draw in its breath and another six to let it out. This explained why there were high tides and low tides, twice each day!

Retold from George Douglas (ed.), *Scottish Fairy and Folk Tales*, 1893, and Ernest W. Marwick, *The Folklore of Orkney and Shetland*, 1975.

The *quetzal* is a bird that lives in the remote, cloud-covered rain forests of southern Mexico and Guatemala. The male bird has two extraordinarily long tail feathers which ripple behind him as he flies. With the slightest movement, they shimmer and change colour from shades of green through to blue. *Coatl* means snake. Thus Quetzalcoatl is a bird-snake. But he is more usually called a feathered snake or plumed serpent. He is primarily a wind god and creator. The supreme god's name is Texcatlipoca, which means Smoking Mirror.

Quetzalcoatl is the dominant decorative motif in the ancient buildings of the high plateaux of Mexico. Some sculptures depict him as a great swirl of long, reed-like feathers with a snake's head emerging from the top. A human face is sometimes framed within his open jaws, while hands and feet can be glimpsed among the feathers.

Birds' feathers were used by the Aztecs to make superb cloaks and head-dresses. The most valued feathers and featherwork were called 'shadows of the Sacred Ones'.

This story is based on a poem from a sixteenth-century manuscript, in Nahuatl, the language of the Aztecs and the Toltecs before them. For an English translation see C. Burland, I. Nicholson, H. Osborne, *Mythology of the Americas*, 1970.

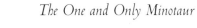

The One and Only Minotaur

 The story of the Minotaur, though generally termed a Greek myth, probably recalls something of the traditions of the much earlier, great Cretan civilization. The first palace at Knossos was built about 1900 BC and for the next five hundred years, as each palace was destroyed by earthquake or fire, another was built on top. Archaeologists have discovered bull decorations throughout the palace – bulls' heads, bulls' horns and a vivid wall-painting depicting the sport of bull-jumping, which happened every springtime. Acrobats, both young men and young women, had to seize a charging bull by the horns, turn somersaults over his back and land on the ground behind. Ancient Egyptian gods and goddesses often had a human body with an animal head, such as a cat, a hawk or - like the Minotaur – a bull.

Three Fabulous Eggs

Nagas can change shape – one moment they can be a hooded snake, the next human, or, as shown in some stone carvings, human from the waist up. Usually they are gentle. But if angered they are able, with a single glance, to turn a person to ashes. Female Nagas (sometimes called Nagini) are beautiful and may marry a human.

All Nagas love jewels, especially rubies. They live underwater or underground in jewel-studded palaces full of treasures, flowers, singing and dancing. They are god-like beings, and are important in Hindu and Buddhist myths and art throughout much of India, and also in countries further east such as Java, Cambodia and, as in this story, Burma.

Retold from Maung Htin Aung, *Burmese Folktales*, 1948.

Bird of the Sun

The Phoenix is the Greek name for the mythical Egyptian bird the Bennu. Both names mean "palm tree". It is the only bird of its kind, and is a symbol of the sun. It lives east of Egypt, either in Arabia or India. Writers disagree about how long the bird lives, but five hundred years is the commonest opinion.

See R. Van Den Broek (translated by I. Seeger), *The Myth of the Phoenix*, 1972.

Rio de la
Plata
Barras dos Castellanes